This book belongs to

For Rupert and Erin
(And with thanks to Peter Perspective)
C.F.

First published in Great Britain in 2011 by Gullane Children's Books, 185 Fleet Street, London EC4A 2HS

ISBN 978-0-545-39052-1

12 11 10 9 8 7 6 5 4 3 2 1   11 12 13 14 15 16/0

Printed in the U.S.A.   08

First Scholastic printing, September 2011

ASTONISHING ANIMAL
ABC

by Charles Fuge

SCHOLASTIC INC.
New York Toronto London Auckland
Sydney Mexico City New Delhi Hong Kong

A, arty aardvark,

B, bouncing bear,

C, cozy cobra
curled up in a
comfy chair.

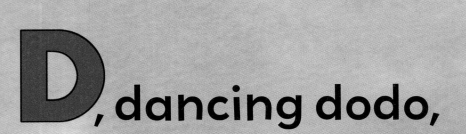

D, dancing dodo,

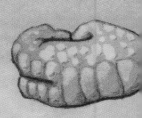

E, enormous egg,

F, fat flamingo feeling frightened, on one leg.

G,
girl gorilla,

H and I,
hare on ice,

J, jolly jackal and his joyful, jumping mice.

K, king koala,

L, lion's lost,

M, mouse at market asking, "What do mammoths cost?"

N, nasty narwhal,

O, outraged owl,

P, pirate penguin
and his panther,
on the prowl.

Q, quite quiet quail,

R, rhinos roar,

S, snoozy sloth needs sleep— why won't they let him snore?

T, tortoise training,

U, unicorn,

V, vulture visits vet (a Viking vole named Vaughn).

x-ray department →

W, worried walrus,

X and **Y**,
x-ray yak,

and **Z** is a zooming...